Bernard Ashley

Your guess is as good as mine

Illustrated by Steven Cain

Julia MacRae Books

a division of Franklin Watts

Text © 1983 Bernard Ashley
Illustrations © 1983 Steven Cain
All rights reserved
First published in Great Britain 1983 by
Julia MacRae Books
A division of Franklin Watts
12a Golden Square, London, W1R 4BA
and Franklin Watts Inc.
387 Park Avenue South, New York 10016.

British Library Cataloguing in Publication Data
Ashley, Bernard
    Your guess is as good as mine – (Redwing Series)
    I.   Title
©823'.914 [J]   PZ7
ISBN 0–86203–132–X UK edition
ISBN 0–531–03765–7 US edition
Library of Congress Catalog Card No: 83–61540

Printed in Great Britain by
Robert Hartnoll, Bodmin

Contents

1

Nicky didn't like this feeling one bit. It made him jumpy, this churning over in his stomach all the time and him not knowing why. Before a big game or a Maths test, all right, he expected it then: but not for no reason, not for just this jittery feeling that if he started something he might not finish it: or that something he didn't like was going to happen.

He came out of the school building and looked up at the sky. Perhaps those black clouds that had hung as low as treetops all day had something to do with it. Well, if so, it'd be a good job when it made up its mind to rain. He'd had enough of the jumps.

It had been one of those days all through:

1

nothing normal about it. Games had been called off because of that dark sky over the marshes, Lee was away with something so there were no laughs to be had, and there was nothing to look forward to on the telly that night. He took a deep breath and blew out his disgust. He'd probably end up reading a book! Well, at least someone else's jitters might cheer him up. Yes, tucked up in bed with his spy book – that wouldn't be so bad. Then it'd be switch off the light and hope Lee was back tomorrow.

He looked up into the gloom again, at the signboard above the school gate. But he wasn't in the mood to jump at it tonight. Let the flaky old paint of *Mrs A. Bottomley* be, for today. There was tomorrow and all the year to wear the letters off at both ends and turn it into a laugh. It wasn't the same fun without Lee – and, besides, tonight wasn't a night to hang about.

So, on he went out of the gate and into the street. He brushed his hand half-heartedly into the dusty hedge of the caretaker's garden: but there wasn't even a web, let alone a spider. All the signs seemed to be saying get home fast. It was definitely one of those get-it-over days.

Rachel Power jumped at the board Nicky had passed and followed him out of the school, keeping a safe ten metres behind. She'd catch him up when he was past that spider hedge. He was usually a good laugh, was Nicky. They'd always walked home together, before Lee came: you just had to look out for his tricks, that was all. Spiders down your neck – and brilliant, he was, at kiss chase.

"Nicky!" she shouted.

But a car came past and he didn't seem to hear. She opened her mouth again. But a cold and sudden plop on the back of her neck put paid to a second shout. An attack of large, splashing drops began hitting the pavement all round her, quickly covering the ground with a pattern of black to match the sky.

She ran. Everyone ran. It was screams and
running feet all along the street, especially
when the storm began for real. Every head
was down, everyone's eyes too busy with the
slippery slabs and sudden kerbs to give much
thought to what was happening to anyone else.
And Rachel with the rest. She saw things she
wouldn't remember till later, like lucky Nicky
getting a lift in his dad's car – and something
being funny about it and all – but she didn't
take any of it in as she made her wet dash for

home. It was all too drenching for that – and coming in wet and making work for your mum was something you tried hard not to do. Against that there wasn't a lot that really mattered, not Nicky, not funny cars, not anything . . .

The rain hit Nicky hard, sting, slap, smack around the head, as if he were in a fight with his big brother. There had to be hail in this lot if it was coming down hard enough to hurt, he thought. And was that a rumble of thunder? If it was, there was lightning about, and you could get hurt worse than by hail with all those millions of volts frizzing down. A cold cube of fear suddenly froze up his stomach. That rotten feeling he'd had all day of something bad happening. Was it this? Was it a storm he had to watch out for?

And then he knew. Or he thought he knew. Like some gigantic light being switched on, a wide white flash streaked across the sky. It lit the undersides of things and wiped out every shadow. And in the same stopped heart-beat a

crack like something blowing up banged
around the streets, shook the sides of houses
and rattled at the glass.

Everybody screamed. Everybody ran. And
Nicky shouted, certain the thing was meant for
him. Everything had been building up to this,
then, to him being one of those unlucky
ones-in-a-million you read about in the papers.
"Mum! Mum!" In that instant he didn't care
who heard him, Rachel Power, little kids . . .
He was scared stiff, and he'd never wanted to
be safe inside somewhere so badly in all his life.

It seemed too good to be true when he saw
the yellow Mini standing there: his dad having
the sense to bring the car round. But his jump
for joy lost its heart before his feet got back to
the ground. Their Mini was up on blocks in the
garden, wasn't it, and this had different rust,
and a different number. Same colour, though.
Just his rotten luck! A lift home could make all
the difference in this storm, where even the rain
was that soaking stuff like a proper shower at
the baths – and still hitting him as if it meant it.
Nicky put his head down again.

"Quick, get out of this lot! Hop in, son."

The car door opened, and for a second Nicky was confused. It wasn't their car, he knew that, and yet . . . Why . . .? He stopped and looked into it.

"Come on, don't hang about. You want to stay out in this storm?"

A man was holding the door open from the inside, respectable looking, smiling just a bit, but with that take-it-or-leave-it look that said it was just a friendly offer in the storm, say yes quick or he'd shut the door and drive off.

Nicky's heart was still thumping with the fright of that sudden flash. Around him the screams and the footsteps had gone as others had shot off to safety somewhere. All he could see at that moment were those four rubber tyres between the man and the road, while in his head he heard his father's words when they'd been caught in the car by a storm. "You're safe as houses in here, Nicky. We're insulated . . ."

Nicky looked back at the man.

"Quick, then, if you're coming. You know

me, don't you? We must live near, I've seen you around."

Nicky screwed up his eyes in the rain. Now he'd said it, the man did have a face he thought he knew – and he was very smart in a clean, white raincoat, with his shirt collar done up and a tie on.

"Lucky I was passing, with this lot throwing itself down."

Another flash filled the sky, another bang seemed to shake the car. In the white light the man looked kindly at Nicky, straight, open, not pushing things.

"But I haven't got all day, you know. Anyway, you're wet already and you don't seem to mind the lightning, so perhaps you're not bothered . . ." He started to close the door.

And that made Nicky's mind up. Someone you couldn't trust would have tried a lot harder to get him into the car, wouldn't he? Not only that, now he was dead sure he knew that face.

"Hold on!" Nicky said. "Thanks." He got in, into the back past the tip-up seat. "25 Tilbury,

9

I live."

"I know, I know," the man laughed. He put the car into gear and checked carefully in the off-side mirror. "25 Tilbury, it is."

Rachel Power stood dripping water into a
growing pool on the kitchen floor.

"You stupid girl," her mother said, "coming
in like this. Look at my tiles. You're soaking
wet!"

"Well, I couldn't come in dry. It's pouring
down of rain!"

"As if I'm not up to my eyes already. Look at
these clothes. Ruined! Do you think money for
clothes grows on trees? You could've took
shelter, couldn't you?"

"Where?"

"Back in school, for a start."

"No chance. Them cleaners moan more'n you
do!"

Wet smacks hurt worse than dry, and the one
Rachel got made her jump and shout as Mrs
Power started tugging the clothes over her head.

"You'll remember tonight, my girl!" she
said. "Little madam! You mark my words!"

The car Nicky was in had started to pick up
speed. The man was saying nothing, giving
everything to the road: kept on looking in his
mirrors and peering through the slashing wipers.

Nicky knew driving was hard in this rain, knew the man had to concentrate; but he also knew they were going much too fast on a road this wet; well, faster than his dad would go, anyway. And there was no sense racing, because he only lived round the corner. He looked past the driver's balding head and squinted to see the end of his street. At this speed they'd go flying past if they weren't careful.

"It's just down here, next on the right."

"Eh?"

"My street. You know, Tilbury. Look there!" Nicky's voice rose to a shout as the car swished on past his turning at something over forty miles an hour. "You've missed it. I said . . . Look, go down this next one."

But the car kept on going, and the man at the wheel looked as if he didn't even want to slow down.

"You've gone past the next one and all!"

"That's all right. Don't get worried, son. I've just had an idea, that's all. Being wet. A bit of a surprise, something to tell your teacher about,

won't take long. Then I'll have you home in no
time.''

He had that little laugh in his voice, the one
his uncle had when he came in holding
something secret behind his back. But what
surprise could this bloke have in the rain that
wouldn't take five minutes? It didn't sound
right, somehow.

"*Where* do you live?" Nicky asked.

"Not far. You must've seen me in the shops,
or somewhere. I know you."

"Do you know my name?" Nicky's voice

14

sounded strange, even to himself; like in a
room without an echo.

"Eh? What's that, son?"

That 'son' again. Is that really all he could
call him? 'Son' was a label Nicky hated from
anyone except his mum and dad.

Meanwhile another side street went by, and
another, with the man hunched more and more
over his wheel.

"Will you stop now, please? I think I want to
get out."

Nicky leaned over the seat, but the man only

15

laughed, as if it was all a bit of fun and Nicky just wasn't in on the secret. "Hey, don't get yourself all het up. I told you, it's a surprise. You'll see. Wouldn't want to spoil it for me, would you?"

"What's my name, then? Just tell me my name, if you know me." Nicky felt his throat getting tight.

"Don't have to know your name to know you, do I? Do you know the names of all the neighbours in your street?" He gave a quick look round at him and smiled. "Here, you're not scared of me, are you?" And he laughed again, as if that was something impossible.

"No, but . . ." It seemed a shame to hurt the man's feelings – it was just that they were going further and further away from home, the streets all flashing past in the spray, till this wasn't even the long way round any more.

"I'll tell you what. Have a sweet. Boys do still like sweets, don't they?"

With his free hand the man pulled down the little door of the glove compartment.

Nicky stared. He'd never seen so many

packets and bars crammed into such a small space before.

"I've got a sweet tooth, too. There should be something in there you like."

"Well, just tell me where we're going, then."

The man banged both his hands on the steering wheel, like Nicky's father did when he was fed up in heavy traffic. "All right, spoil the surprise." He took out a Mars Bar and lobbed it gently into the back. "Just down to the marshes. Not all that far."

Nicky's mother hardly got a word out before
Mrs Power dragged her into the kitchen. "What
do you do with kids like this?" she asked.
"Look at those clothes! Wouldn't you credit a
girl that age with more sense than to run home
in that storm?"

Rachel stood looking sheepish in her pyjamas.
There was no need to make her disgrace all
public to Nicky's mum.

Mrs Davis stared at the pants, socks and frock
heaped up wet in the sink, looking like a little
pile of clothing someone might have found out
in the open.

"I only wish my Nicky had run home," she
said, "wet, dry or covered in muck. But I don't

know *where* he is, Mrs Power. I've rung the school and they said he came out with your Rachel." Her eyes begged for some news.

"He's gone in with a mate, love. Found the dry. Always had more up top, your boy. You haven't given him long, have you?"

"It's just, he never does that. He knows . . ."

"He never went in with a mate." Both the women turned to look at Rachel, who, knowing what Nicky had done, could afford to fold her arms and look smug. "He went off in his dad's car. His dad picked him up. I saw him."

"His dad? He can't have." Mrs Davis frowned. "The car's laid up, been out the front for a month, and his dad's as much up the wall over him as I am."

"But I saw it. Yellow Mini, isn't it? I know the colour. Didn't actually see his dad, but I definitely saw Nicky getting in it. I know 'cos I saw the number, would've had a laugh if it hadn't been so wet . . ." Rachel looked from one to the other as if they wouldn't understand. "See, it's a sort of a joke we've got . . . an' that number . . ."

19

Mrs Davis grabbed hold of Mrs Power's arm. "Could your Rachel throw some things on and come back with me?" she pleaded. "Please? Tell Mr Davis all about this car?"

Mrs Power looked a bit put out with having to release Rachel from her punishment, but she nodded. "All right, if you like. Put your mac on, Rachel – and come straight back. But this had better not be one of your airy-fairy stories, madam!" The look she gave to Rachel promised another good smack if it was. "We're none of us in the mood for jokes tonight."

Once round the corner, the look on Rachel's face said she wished she'd never seen anything. Or never said anything about it, anyway.

They were on the Davises' doorstep. Nicky's mother wasn't waiting till they got inside: she grabbed her husband as he opened the door.

"Rachel saw a yellow car. Like ours. Nicky getting into it – and something funny about it."

"Getting into it?" Mr Davis threw his cigarette into the garden.

"She reckons you picked Nicky up from

school just when the rain came on."

Mr Davis looked at Rachel. "In that?" He waved at the yellow Mini on the grass. It was sitting up on its blocks with water dripping from where the wheels weren't. "How could I pick him up in that?"

Rachel stared at the stranded vehicle. She felt awkward now, under attack in a strange way, but with nothing actually being said. At least she knew where she stood with her mum's hard line. She looked at the rusting bodywork, trying to find something useful to say.

"Well?" There was more than a hint of disbelief in Mr Davis's voice.

"I don't know . . ." But now Rachel looked at the number plate, dim and dirty, and . . . "Hey! Yours *is* a different number. The other one, like I said, it was funny . . . I remember seeing it . . ." Her mind went back to that quick look in the rain, that something about the car number that she'd wanted to tell someone.

"That other one. It was L E Y something. The same as we're trying to rub off *Bottomley* on the school sign." She went red, almost ashamed to admit their baby trick of trying to make it say *A Bottom*. "That's why I noticed it."

"Nine, nine, nine!" Mrs Davis was pulling hard at her husband's arm. "Nine, nine, nine!" she shouted.

"I didn't see the number," said Rachel, "only L E Y."

"No – nine, nine, nine, *police*!" Mrs Davis ran into the living room. "Our Nicky's gone off in a car with someone, some stranger!"

But her shaking fingers couldn't find the holes in the telephone, and Nicky's father had to pull it out of her hands and do it for her.

If the sky had seemed low before, down on the marshes it was close enough to touch. The rain had stopped, but a clam in the air like wet flannels round the face hit Nicky as the car door opened.

His spirits had fallen with the sky. He'd felt so helpless in the car. Like a bad ride at the fair, it had been, when there was no stopping the roundabout however much you screamed and shouted, because that was what people were supposed to do. Not that Nicky had done that. The last thing he wanted was for the man to think he was scared. But he had wanted the car to stop, and he had wanted to be let out where lots of people were.

24

Now they were here on the marshes: and all at once the car seemed a safer place to be.

All the way there Nicky had known he couldn't reach the door from the back. Not to get out. His own car was the same. And even if he could, there'd been no stopping anywhere, not even at cross roads. The man had seemed to time it so that the car never even slowed down.

Or was all that in Nicky's mind? Was he being all dramatic like his mother sometimes said he was? The man had still sounded gentle and nice. He'd laughed and joked and kept on giving him sweets. But he wouldn't say another word about what sort of surprise he'd got, however many ways Nicky had tried to ask.

Now they were down by the river, and the car had stopped in a farmer's gate. And all there was to see was sky and water and marsh: and the only living things were several silly sheep who ran away as soon as the car had stopped.

"Come on, son," the man said firmly. "Nearly there. Time to get out."

Nicky had never felt so alone. No-one came

spend his life there if he could."

"Where, love, where?"

Nobody blinked.

"Down on the marshes. By the old range. Wonderful sights, he's seen down there . . ."

But as she drew breath to tell them of those wonders, the race began: an obstacle over the chairs to the door, and a head-down sprint to the police car in the street.

down here to play. Half a mile upstream the bigger boys went fishing, and further down they looked for old bottles. But here it was just boggy marsh all the way to the river, and the old army rifle range in between. Apart from the sheep that was all it was fit for: shooting bullets into things.

The man took Nicky by the wrist and helped him out of the car. "Come on, over here."

"Where? Where we going? I want to go home."

"Don't be daft! Just you wait till you see . . ." The man's raincoat flapped and his wispy hair blew all ways as he bent his body into the wind and started walking them fast across the rough, wet ground.

"You stop it! Let me go! I don't want to come. I want to go home!" Nicky pulled at the arm and tried to dig his heels in.

"Now don't you be silly. I'll take you home all right. A surprise I said, didn't I? Well, a surprise you're going to have. You've come this far, haven't you?" The man's voice was raised above the whine of the marsh wind as he gripped Nicky's wrist harder and pulled him on again.

"Let go! You're hurting!" But Nicky's voice hardly reached his own ears.

"Stupid, you'll get lost out here if you run. Come on, nearly there." The man was shouting, pointing with his free hand and pulling him hard towards the lines of soldiers' trenches.

And now Nicky knew for sure. The man *was* one of those they warned you about. He'd got hold of him too hard, his voice was too rough – and he was pulling him towards the trenches. What proper surprise could anyone have down there?

"Stop it! *Stop*! Let me go!"

Nicky twisted his wrist to get out of the grip. He bit at the big sleeve, kicked at the long legs – but the man's strong grip didn't loosen, and he was being half-pulled and half-carried towards the second trench.

"You wanna get lost? Now you stop all that!" the man snapped. "Or you'll start getting me cross, boy!"

Nicky looked at him with wide, terrified

28

eyes: because now a new face went w⟨ith a⟩ new voice, and all the man's pretence a⟨nd⟩ niceness had gone.

Two policemen filled the small front roo⟨m like⟩ grown-ups in a Wendy house.

"How did you know my son lived her⟨e?" the⟩ old lady asked them. "He's never had any dealings with the police before."

"On the computer, radio'd through to u⟨s. A⟩ bit of his number plate and the make of his ⟨car.⟩ It is your son's car, isn't it?"

"It must be if you say it is. Why, what's ⟨he⟩ supposed to have done?"

One of the policemen sat in a chair. "Noth⟨ing,⟩ missus, if we're in time . . ."

". . . If you can help us find him, quick. Lik⟨e,⟩ are there any favourite places he goes to . . .?"

The old lady frowned and touched the tea-p⟨ot⟩ no-one had time for. "Well, if he's not at work . . ."

"He's not at work."

"Then the only place he goes is bird watching. He loves it, he's quite an expert. He'd

29

5

"Ouch!" Nicky pretended to fall. It was the last trick he knew to play. "My ankle!" What the mother birds did, the broken wing: something he'd read in a book somewhere.

"Come on, sonny! Stop playing me up."

The man was really angry now and trying to pull him down into one of the trenches, well out of sight of the road. Which meant Nicky had only one last possible chance. Stay up here on the flat, if he could . . .

"I can't go no further. I've broke my ankle." He sank with all his weight on one side to the ground.

"Come on, get up, who d'you think you're kidding?"

31

The man tugged at him; but with Nicky on the ground he had to alter his feet, shift his grip, let go for half a second. And, suddenly, there was the chance. Like 'releaso'! A lifetime's practice in the playground suddenly paid off. Nicky dug in his toes, and pushed, and ran for his life away from the man's reach and towards the river. He put down his head and thrust all his energy into his clammy, wet legs.

And all the man did was laugh. A low and throaty laugh which even the wind couldn't get at. I'll catch you, it seemed to say, I'll catch you, son. There's no getting away from me.

But Nicky tried. He stumbled and tripped on the hillocky ground, he whipped his face in the reed-grass, his ankle went over for real. But he ran as the laugh came after him, and he kept on running after the laugh had stopped. Cold marsh air filled his lungs, and his throat burned hotter than hell. Wind seared his eyes as he stared at the river, a hammer seemed to thud at his heart. He was going the wrong way, he knew he was: the wrong way, away from the gate and the road.

But getting away from the man came first!
Away anywhere. Into a cluster of thin bushes.
Zig-zag in and out, keep them between him and
the man, dodge and run. He grabbed a prickly
handful out of his way and looked for him.
There was no sign. The marsh behind him was
as dead as the moon. And there was the nearest
trench: twenty metres away: get round the end
of that and away up the other side and then the
man could get lost – *he'd* be back at the road!

A quick last look. All clear still. Had the
bloke given up when he saw the run Nicky had
in him? Please, Mum, yes! Then leg it for home!
To the end of that trench and round it – now!

Nicky spurted – and suddenly sprang into
the air in terror as a loud footstep splashed
centimetres behind him and hard breathing
wheezed close to his head.

"Come here, you young fool!"

God! He was . . .! How could . . .!? Without
thinking, Nicky threw his body forward, jerked
his head to his waist to avoid the clutch. Help!
could he still make it to the other side of the
trench and turn the chase – bolt for the road

before the maniac got him?

Nicky shut his eyes. A last desperate push, away from those hands —

And down! All at once his feet had gone from under him and he was doing a mad dance in space, clutching at nothing, dirt in his mouth — landing with a sickening thud to sprawl flat in the bottom of an overgrown slit trench.

He was winded, stunned, his chest hurt and he had to claw mud from his eyes. But he stumbled to his feet. He had to keep going, he knew. There were no second chances in this deadly game of chase. But which way was he facing? Which way to go now?

Who cared which way? Just run! He banged and grazed himself on the crumbling wall. Sheer panic drove him on along the trench.

But he heard the thump as the man dropped down behind him: down here where no-one would see them. Just where he'd wanted him! And then the footsteps again, heavy, determined to get him.

But there was an end to the trench. Nicky could see it. If he could get there in time, climb down here to play. Half a mile upstream the bigger boys went fishing, and further down they looked for old bottles. But here it was just boggy marsh all the way to the river, and the old army rifle range in between. Apart from the sheep that was all it was fit for: shooting bullets into things.

The man took Nicky by the wrist and helped him out of the car. "Come on, over here."

"Where? Where we going? I want to go home."

"Don't be daft! Just you wait till you see . . ." The man's raincoat flapped and his wispy hair blew all ways as he bent his body into the wind and started walking them fast across the rough, wet ground.

"You stop it! Let me go! I don't want to come. I want to go home!" Nicky pulled at the arm and tried to dig his heels in.

"Now don't you be silly. I'll take you home all right. A surprise I said, didn't I? Well, a surprise you're going to have. You've come this far, haven't you?" The man's voice was raised above the whine of the marsh wind as he

27

gripped Nicky's wrist harder and pulled him on again.

"Let go! You're hurting!" But Nicky's voice hardly reached his own ears.

"Stupid, you'll get lost out here if you run. Come on, nearly there." The man was shouting, pointing with his free hand and pulling him hard towards the lines of soldiers' trenches.

And now Nicky knew for sure. The man *was* one of those they warned you about. He'd got hold of him too hard, his voice was too rough – and he was pulling him towards the trenches. What proper surprise could anyone have down there?

"Stop it! *Stop*! Let me go!"

Nicky twisted his wrist to get out of the grip. He bit at the big sleeve, kicked at the long legs – but the man's strong grip didn't loosen, and he was being half-pulled and half-carried towards the second trench.

"You wanna get lost? Now you stop all that!" the man snapped. "Or you'll start getting me cross, boy!"

Nicky looked at him with wide, terrified

28

eyes: because now a new face went w.
new voice, and all the man's pretence ¿
niceness had gone.

Two policemen filled the small front roo
grown-ups in a Wendy house.

"How did you know my son lived her¢
old lady asked them. "He's never had any
dealings with the police before."

"On the computer, radio'd through to u:
bit of his number plate and the make of his
It is your son's car, isn't it?"

"It must be if you say it is. Why, what's l
supposed to have done?"

One of the policemen sat in a chair. "Nothi
missus, if we're in time . . ."

". . . If you can help us find him, quick. Lik
are there any favourite places he goes to . . .?"

The old lady frowned and touched the tea-po
no-one had time for. "Well, if he's not at
work . . ."

"He's not at work."

"Then the only place he goes is bird watching. He loves it, he's quite an expert. He'd

29

spend his life there if he could."

"Where, love, where?"

Nobody blinked.

"Down on the marshes. By the old range.
Wonderful sights, he's seen down there . . ."

But as she drew breath to tell them of those
wonders, the race began: an obstacle over the
chairs to the door, and a head-down sprint to
the police car in the street.

30

before the maniac got him?

Nicky shut his eyes. A last desperate push, away from those hands –

And down! All at once his feet had gone from under him and he was doing a mad dance in space, clutching at nothing, dirt in his mouth – landing with a sickening thud to sprawl flat in the bottom of an overgrown slit trench.

He was winded, stunned, his chest hurt and he had to claw mud from his eyes. But he stumbled to his feet. He had to keep going, he knew. There were no second chances in this deadly game of chase. But which way was he facing? Which way to go now?

Who cared which way? Just run! He banged and grazed himself on the crumbling wall. Sheer panic drove him on along the trench.

But he heard the thump as the man dropped down behind him: down here where no-one would see them. Just where he'd wanted him! And then the footsteps again, heavy, determined to get him.

But there was an end to the trench. Nicky could see it. If he could get there in time, climb

But getting away from the man came first!
Away anywhere. Into a cluster of thin bushes.
Zig-zag in and out, keep them between him and
the man, dodge and run. He grabbed a prickly
handful out of his way and looked for him.
There was no sign. The marsh behind him was
as dead as the moon. And there was the nearest
trench: twenty metres away: get round the end
of that and away up the other side and then the
man could get lost – *he'd* be back at the road!

A quick last look. All clear still. Had the
bloke given up when he saw the run Nicky had
in him? Please, Mum, yes! Then leg it for home!
To the end of that trench and round it – now!

Nicky spurted – and suddenly sprang into
the air in terror as a loud footstep splashed
centimetres behind him and hard breathing
wheezed close to his head.

"Come here, you young fool!"

God! He was . . .! How could . . .!? Without
thinking, Nicky threw his body forward, jerked
his head to his waist to avoid the clutch. Help!
could he still make it to the other side of the
trench and turn the chase – bolt for the road

The man tugged at him; but with Nicky on the ground he had to alter his feet, shift his grip, let go for half a second. And, suddenly, there was the chance. Like 'releaso'! A lifetime's practice in the playground suddenly paid off. Nicky dug in his toes, and pushed, and ran for his life away from the man's reach and towards the river. He put down his head and thrust all his energy into his clammy, wet legs.

And all the man did was laugh. A low and throaty laugh which even the wind couldn't get at. I'll catch you, it seemed to say, I'll catch you, son. There's no getting away from me.

But Nicky tried. He stumbled and tripped on the hillocky ground, he whipped his face in the reed-grass, his ankle went over for real. But he ran as the laugh came after him, and he kept on running after the laugh had stopped. Cold marsh air filled his lungs, and his throat burned hotter than hell. Wind seared his eyes as he stared at the river, a hammer seemed to thud at his heart. He was going the wrong way, he knew he was: the wrong way, away from the gate and the road.

32

"Ouch!" Nicky pretended to fall. It was the last trick he knew to play. "My ankle!" What the mother birds did, the broken wing: something he'd read in a book somewhere.

"Come on, sonny! Stop playing me up."

The man was really angry now and trying to pull him down into one of the trenches, well out of sight of the road. Which meant Nicky had only one last possible chance. Stay up here on the flat, if he could . . .

"I can't go no further. I've broke my ankle." He sank with all his weight on one side to the ground.

"Come on, get up, who d'you think you're kidding?"

31

out before . . .

The black mud favoured light feet, and for those last few seconds Nicky thought he had just the ghost of a chance – if he could only climb far enough up that trench end to kick at the hands which'd grab at his legs.

One last effort! There'd never be another chance, not ever in his life. The end of the trench was the end of the chase.

Nicky got there, shut his ears to what was coming as he leapt at the soil, scrambled like an animal to the rim above his head. He put his life on every thin blade of grass fingers could find. He kicked. He scrabbled. He screamed at where he wanted to be as if screaming would somehow get him there.

And then he saw it. Above him. Looming above. The big black shape. The man! Who'd got out, gone round, cut him off.

"No!" yelled Nicky. "No! You . . .!"

The hand grabbing down was big and wet. But there was never any chance of slipping that grip. The time for slips and mistakes was over.

"Come on, my son, I've got you," the policeman said: and that 'my son' was the most welcome sound in all the world to Nicky. "You're a lucky little devil, I'll tell you!"

He was lifted out to the sound of shouting back in the trench – of which Nicky heard nothing as he heaved for breath and stood shaking with the end of his efforts.

All the way across the hundred metres of stumbling footsteps, over to the road and the cars clustered round the yellow Mini, Nicky kept himself dry-eyed and dignified in the

36

policeman's arms: right up to the moment he saw his parents drive up. And then everyone seemed to cry, and a word was as hard to get out as a hair in the mouth. But out it came in the end. The relief, the thanks to sharp-eyed

Rachel, to the police computer and the speed of a radio-controlled car. And then, because they had to be said, a few soft words of reproach.

"You should never have done it, Nicky."

"Never go off with *anyone*. How many times have we told you?"

"It doesn't matter *what* they say."

"There are more sick people about than there are bolts of lightning heading for you. You should've gone back in school, Nicky. There are people you can trust there."

Nicky nodded. There was no excuse. He'd been stupid, he knew that – and a lucky little devil, like the policeman said.

"You know what his story was?" Nicky's father asked.

"No?" Nicky put a thumb in his book. He wanted to know. He'd had a bad time, but he could cope with talking about it now – here in the safety of his bedroom where all that had happened seemed so unreal.

"He reckons he had a nest to show you. Something any kid would give his eye-teeth to

see, he said. A heron's or something, down on
the river's edge: very rare, on the ground, with
the mother on her eggs in the rain.''

"Do they believe him?''

"He showed them the nest, all right. And
back home he's got binoculars and books on it,
and everything.''

39

Nicky closed his eyes. He tried to go back over what had happened: tried to remember exactly what had been said. It was true he hadn't been threatened, except with getting lost. He hadn't been *told* anything, and nothing had actually been *done* to him, had it? So had it just been him? Had he been scared out of his life for nothing? Would it all have been all right if he hadn't panicked and run?

He didn't think so.

He opened his eyes again and looked at his dad.

"Do *you* believe him? Do you reckon he was . . . going to . . . you know?"

Mr Davis sat silent for a moment. "*I* don't know," he said. He looked at the spy story Nicky was holding. "Life's a lot more complicated than that sort of thing makes out, you know. Like, has it struck you that guy doesn't even know himself what he was going to do . . .?"

Nicky stared at his dad: somehow, that made it all sound even worse, the man not knowing, acting no different to some kid.

40

"No, mate, I couldn't tell you. And the chances are, he couldn't, either. So your guess is as good as mine . . ."

Nicky shivered: slid down into his bed. This wasn't the way it should have been, this not being sure, this still feeling jumpy. There was only one thing for it: get the light out, get to sleep, quick, get today over and done with, Nicky thought: and keep his fingers crossed that the only jumps he had tomorrow would be the ones he wanted – up at the L E Y of *Bottomley* on the school sign.